Anonymous

An Account of the Organization & Proceedings of the Battle of Lake Erie Monument Association

SALZWASSER
VERLAG

Anonymous

An Account of the Organization & Proceedings of the Battle of Lake Erie Monument Association

Reprint of the original, first published in 1858.

1st Edition 2023 | ISBN: 978-3-37513-996-4

Verlag (Publisher): Salzwasser Verlag GmbH, Zeilweg 44, 60439 Frankfurt, Deutschland
Vertretungsberechtigt (Authorized to represent): E. Roepke, Zeilweg 44, 60439 Frankfurt, Deutschland
Druck (Print): Books on Demand GmbH, In de Tarpen 42, 22848 Norderstedt, Deutschland

AN ACCOUNT

OF THE

ORGANIZATION & PROCEEDINGS OF THE

BATTLE OF LAKE ERIE

Monument Association.

AND

Celebration of the 45th Anniversary

OF THE

BATTLE OF LAKE ERIE,

AT PUT-IN-BAY ISLAND, ON SEPTEMBER TENTH, 1858.

SANDUSKY:
PRINTED BY HENRY D. COOKE & COMPANY.
1858.

ORIGIN AND ORGANIZATION.

In the year 1852, five companies of the Volunteer Militia of Ohio decided to celebrate the Anniversary of American Independence, by holding a three days' encampment on the renowned and beautiful Island of "Put-in-Bay."

This spot was chosen by them as being, above all others in their vicinity, the most national, and entitled to preference, from the glorious associations with which it is identified, and worthy the commemoration of that most hallowed of American days.

They were composed of the following finely equipped and disciplined companies:

Bay City Guards—Capt. R. R. McMeens.
Sandusky Yagers—Capt. Louis Traub.
Sandusky Artillery—Capt. L. A. Silva.
Washington Guards—Capt. William Lang.
Tiffin Artillery—Capt. Bagby.

The Island was generously surrendered to the service and control of the military, by the gentlemanly proprietor, Col. A. P. Edwards, and placed in the charge of Capt. R. R. McMeens, who was chosen commandant for the occasion.

The weather, during the whole period of the encampment, was one of unclouded sunshine, rendered deliciously cool and exhilirating by the gentle breezes constantly wafted from the broad and blue bosom of the Lake.

On the morning of the 4th, (it being Sabbath,) the Battalion was reviewed by Maj. Gen. Isaac A. Mills, and his aid, Col. A. A. Camp, and presented a very martial and imposing appearance; after which, an appropriate and eloquent discourse was delivered by the Rev. E. R. Jewett.

This was the first military display, encampment or celebration ever held on the Island since the time it was occupied by Gen. Harrison's army.

On Monday, the 5th, "*the day*" was celebrated. A national salute was fired at sunrise; immense crowds of citizens from the opposite shore began to arrive, by steamers and sail craft; and in the afternoon an eloquent oration was delivered by Horatio Wildman, Esq.

During the first trip of the Steamer Arrow from Sandusky to the Island, a preliminary meeting was held, for the purpose of effecting a monumental organization, at which the Rev. Dr. Bronson was chosen Chairman, and Henry D. Cooke Secretary. On motion of Pitt Cooke, Esq., a committee of five was appointed "to draft resolutions expressive of the sense of the meeting, in reference to the erection of a monument on Gibraltar Rock, Put-in-Bay, commemorative of Perry's brilliant victory on Lake Erie, and in honor of the dead who fell in that memo-rable engagement."

Whereupon, Messrs. J. A. Camp, Rev. W. Pitkin, W. F. Stone, Wm. S. Mills and H. D. Cooke were appointed such committee. The meet-ing then adjourned, to give time to the committee to prepare their report. The committee subsequently reported the following resolutions, with an appropriate preamble, which were unanimously adopted:

Resolved, That it is expedient on this day to form an association for the purpose above specified.

Resolved, That these proceedings shall be submitted to the considera-tion and concurrence of those assembled on Put-in-Bay Island.

On motion of W. F. Stone, the Secretary of the meeting was deputed to lay the proceedings of this meeting before the Assembly at Put-in-Bay, for further action.

In pursuance of the last resolution, the proceedings of the meeting on board the Arrow were laid before the vast concourse in the grove on Put-in-Bay Island, who fully concurred in the action of the preliminary meeting, and a committee, consisting of Messrs. J. A. Camp, Wm. S. Mills and Henry D. Cooke, were appointed to draft a preamble and constitution, for the proposed association.

In the afternoon another meeting was called, for the purpose of final action—the Rev. E. R. Jewett in the chair. Whereupon, the following Constitution was adopted:

WHEREAS, On the tenth day of September, in the year of our Lord eighteen hundred and thirteen, the gallant seamen and marines of the American Navy, commanded by the heroic Oliver Hazard Perry, ob-tained a glorious victory over the British Squadron on Lake Erie, which victory turned the tide of war, hitherto adverse to our arms, and was the precursor of a series of brilliant triumphs: AND WHEREAS, on that day many bold hearts, for whom a nation grieved, died victorious in the service of their country, and since by their services and death have left their nation in their debt, it is now both the duty and the pleasure of their countrymen, to erect to their memory a monument, which shall exhibit to future generations the appreciation the present entertains of the value of their service and sacrifice. And inasmuch as the scene of the glorious conflict should point the memorial of the triumph, it is both expedient and proper that such monument should be erected on one of the Put-in-Bay Islands of Lake Erie. THEREFORE, The undersigned trusting to the cordial and efficient co-operation of their countrymen throughout this broad land, do form themselves into an Association, for the purpose above set forth, under the style of "THE BATTLE OF LAKE ERIE MONUMENT ASSOCIATION," and do adopt the following

CONSTITUTION.

ARTICLE FIRST.

Any person can become a member of this Association by paying the Treasurer the sum of one dollar.

ARTICLE SECOND.

The officers of the Association shall consist of a President, twenty-five Vice Presidents, a Secretary, an Assistant Secretary and a Treasurer, whose duties shall be such as usually belong to such officers.

ARTICLE THIRD.

The control and management of the property and interests of this Association shall be vested in a Board of Managers, to be elected *viva voce*, any ten of whom, at any regular meeting, shall constitute a quorum. They shall have power to fill vacancies in their own body. They shall have power to elect from their own body an executive committee, to consist of five members, three of whom shall constitute a quorum for the transaction of business, to whom they may depute their authority, and who shall be subject to their control.

The Executive Committee shall have power to call meetings of the Board of Managers, and to name the time and place of meeting.

The especial duty of the Board of Managers is declared to be, to carry into execution the object of this Association.

After the adoption of the Constitution, the meeting proceeded to elect officers, in compliance with its provisions, when

Hon. Lewis Cass was chosen President.

On the list of Vice Presidents, the following gentlemen were chosen:
Col. J. J. Abert, U. S. Topographical Engineers, Washington City;

Hon. Elisha Whittlesey, Commodore R. F. Stockton, General Cadwalader, Philadelphia; Hon. Reuben Wood, Ohio; Maj. John G. Camp, Sandusky; Capt. Stephen Champlin, Buffalo; J. A. Harris, Cleveland; Hon. Judge Burnett, Cincinnati.

A Board of Managers was to be subsequently chosen.

A Provisional Executive Committee was appointed, consisting of Maj. John G. Camp, Hon. E. Cooke, Earl Bill, Esq., Col. A. P. Edwards, and J. A. Harris, Esq., with authority to act until the Board of Managers shall elect an Executive Committee in the manner prescribed by the Constitution, three of whom shall constitute a quorum for doing business.

The meeting then adjourned with three hearty cheers for the proposed monument, and a considerable amount of subscriptions was left with the President.

This great work was then considered to have commenced under the most favorable auspices, and with flattering prospects of future completion. But unfortunately, from the sudden and severe outbreak of cholera throughout the Lake region of country, soon after, the excitement consequent upon the Presidential campaign, as well as the very local character of the celebration, no active or immediate steps were taken to carry its provisions into effect, or complete its further organization, and the whole matter was allowed to subside into a state of indifference and ultimate neglect.

During the past summer, however, the subject was again agitated by those who had become deeply interested in the laudable and patriotic project, and the Hon. E. Cooke, being the only accessible member of the original provisional committee, was waited upon and requested to call a meeting of the committee, and fill, as authorized by the Constitution, the vacancies occasioned by death or otherwise, with the view of reviving the subject, and enlisting all the cities of Lake Erie in a union celebration on the approaching anniversary of the battle.

This was accordingly done, and the following committee appointed: E. COOKE, WM. S. PIERSON, F. S. THORPE, J. A. CAMP, R. R. McMEENS.

The editor of the Commercial Register of Sandusky, was then solicited by the committee, to bring the subject before the attention of the press and people, in order to awaken their patriotism, and insure their hearty co-operation. When in their daily issue of August 13th, the following spirited appeal appeared:

THE TENTH OF SEPTEMBER.

" But few days in American history are more rich in patriotic associations, than the tenth of September, 1813; and at its recollection every truly American heart pulsates with a renewed thrill of patriotic enthusiasm. It is gratifying to note that each succeeding recurrence of the anniversary of the great event, that then transpired, the grand achievement then attained, does not mark a waning in the hallowed regard in which that brilliant victory, and the immortal victors are held by America's loyal sons. We are all proud of that demonstration of our country's triumph over Britain's boasted naval power; we are all proud of our gallant Perry, and point with pride to his imposing prowess, rejoice that he was an American, and enshrine the memory of his glowing deeds of bravery, in the warmest corner of our inner hearts.

"It is a befitting tribute to the memories of those brave spirits who participated in the struggle of that memorable day, and our regard for the importance of the event, that its every anniversary should find the Lake cities, by their delegates assembled as brothers at Put-in-Bay, ground made classic by its nearness to the battle scene, and by its being the urn that holds the sleeping dust of those who fell in freedom's cause, commemorating that event with appropriate exercises, renewing the ties of fraternal good feeling, and re-kindling those fires of patriotism, that burned with such undimned lustre in those brave hearts, that now lie pulseless and still in unknown graves, near the hallowed scene of their glorious death.   *   *   *   *   *   *

"We repeat, then, the approaching tenth of September, will be an appropriate occasion to give this monument association a fresh impetus. Let Buffalonians, Erians, Clevelanders, Sanduskians, Toledoans, and Detroiters, go to Put-in-Bay, prepared to contribute liberally of their means to this glorious work, and let us have a monument erected to commemorate the event which makes prominent the day we celebrate, that will do us honor."

The press along the whole length of the Lake shore, responded to, and reiterated the sentiment with a promptness and zeal most commendable and patriotic, for which the committee feel it their duty to acknowledge the appreciation of their indebtedness, and much of the successful results of the day.

Subsequently the committee deemed it proper to publish the following card, for the purpose of announcing the proposed celebration, and concentrating some definite action thereon.

CARD.
"We have met the enemy and they are ours."

From the spontaneous and favorable responses, of all the leading journals of the Lake cities, on the subject of holding a union celebration a

Put-in-bay Island, on the approaching anniversary of the Battle of Lake Erie, the 10th of Sept. next, to do honor to the memory of the illustrious Perry, and homage to the graves of his illustrious dead, the Executive Committee of the "Battle of Lake Erie Monument Association," instituted on the 4th of July, 1852, have deemed it a proper occasion to invite all patriotic citizens to co-operate with them in adopting the best measures to secure the necessary funds, obtain designs, and insure the construction and early completion of the structure.

The site selected for the Monument, was on Gibraltar Rock, an isolated and commanding islet, where Perry's lookout was stationed, and directly in view of the battle scene. Suitable materials for building can be procured upon the ground, thus rendering its accomplishment feasible with but trifling expense.

Then let Buffalo, Erie, Cleveland, Sandusky, Toledo, Detroit, and all other intervening places, with the adjacent country, come together upon this spot, consecrated to our common glory by the heroic achievements of our countrymen, and unite in erecting over the long neglected dust of the "buried brave," a Monument worthy of their deeds and their death.

The interest of the occasion will be much enhanced by the presence of Dr. Usher Parsons, of Providence, R. I., Capt. Stephen Champlin, of Buffalo, N. Y., Lieut. E. Brownell, of New Port, R. I., and possibly, some others of the few remaining survivors of the battle.

The committee would earnestly request that each of the above places would correspond with them, and assist in the selection of suitable speakers, the appointments of time, the order to be observed on arrival, &c.

E. COOKE,
W. S. PIERSON,
F. S. THORPE, } Executive Committee.
J. A. CAMP,
R. R. McMEENS.

Meetings were held in most of the cities and towns, at which it was resolved to attend, and take part in the celebration; Committees of Conference were appointed, and correspondence had with the Executive Committee, who upon advisement, and for the purpose of securing order and concert of action upon arrival at the Island; issued and forwarded the following circular to such committees, for general observance and government.

CIRCULAR.

Sandusky, Ohio, Sept. 1st, 1858.

Gentlemen:

"'The Provisional Executive Committee of the Battle of Lake Erie Monument Association,' appointed July 4th, 1852, at Put-in-

Bay, in view of obtaining immediate and concert of action, in the brief time allowed for consultation on the 10th inst., respectfully offer the following suggestions:

1st. That the several delegations—where such selections have not heretofore been made—prior to the landing on the Island, select five of their number to act as their Executive Committee, and that the Naval and Revenue officers of the United States service in attendance, each select one or more persons for the same purpose.

2nd. That said Committee meet at the Flag Staff near the dock at 11 A. M.

3rd. That after consultation, a general meeting of all present be held, delegations introduced, and officers of the day chosen, and a report from the Committee be made of a plan for renewing the organization of 1852, or a new organization, for building a Monument on Gibraltar, to commemorate the Battle of Lake Erie.

4th. After the completion of such organization, a National Salute be fired.

Adjourn for one hour, for pic-nic and such other refreshments as each delegation may have provided.

5th. On re-assembling after adjournment, speeches by orators selected for the occasion."

E. COOKE,
WM. S. PIERSON,
F. S. THORPE,   } Executive Committee.
J. A. CAMP,
R. R. McMEENS,

Celebration of the 45th Anniversary of the Battle of Lake Erie, at Put-in-Bay Island, on the tenth of September, 1858.

The celebration of the Battle of Lake Erie, on the 10th of September, 1858, was one of the most imposing and thrilling spectacles, and interesting events, witnessed upon the waters of Lake Erie, since the glorious day of the terrible conflict and brilliant victory itself. Large delegations, with vast crowds of citizens, from most of the large cities, and many of the smaller villages of the Lake, congregated upon the Island, made memorable and immortal, as the harbor of Perry's valiant fleet on the morning of the battle, and as the resting place of his illustrious dead, who fell in that action.

The bay itself presented a most grand and gorgeous pageant, crowded with a fleet of magnificent steamers, sail vessels, and yachts, all decorated with gay colored banners, streamers, and pendants, while a battery of fourteen brazen mouthed cannon, waked the echo's of old Erie with a welcome, that made the bold rocks of Gibraltar tremble with their reverberations.

Veterans were there, who had battled side by side with Perry; old men, who had heard the distant thunder of their guns; statesmen, scholars, soldiers, men, women, and children, all animated and inspired by the soul-stirring scene and associations that surrounded them.

The morning of the day was ushered in with dark and threatening clouds, which while the boats were on their way to the Island, discharged themselves in torrents of rain. But all failed to dampen the ardor of the thousands who had armed themselves with a determination to spend the day in appropriate commemoration of the glorious victory with which it is identified.

But most timely and unexpectedly the rain ceased, and the clouds disappeared as by magic, while the sun shone forth in the full effulgence of his glory, gladdening the hearts of all, and causing the transparent surface of the Lake to sparkle far and wide, in one glow of liquid light.

By half past 12 o'clock, all of the several delegations had reached the bay.

The whole fleet was then composed as follows:

U. S. Steamer Michigan—Commander, Joseph Lanman, U. S. N.

U. S. Revenue Cutter, A. V. Brown—Capt. H. A. Mitchell.

Steamer Forest Queen, Buffalo—Capt. Miller.

Steamer Ocean, Cleveland—Capt. Evans.

Steamer Arrow, Cleveland—Capt. Calverly.

Steamer Queen City, Sandusky—Capt. McBride.

Steamer Island Queen, Port Clinton—Capt. Orr.

Steamer Bay City, Toledo—Capt. Edwards.

Steamer Jersey City, Toledo—Capt. Monroe.

Steamer May Queen, Detroit—Capt. Viger.

Tugs, Niagara and Star.

Yachts E. K. Collins, Cleveland; Monarch of the Glen, Perrysburgh; Morning Star, and Comet.

Twenty other sailing vessels swelled the number of excursionists to not less than eight thousand people.

At one o'clock, the Executive Committees of the several cities, representing the various delegations, met in front of the residence of Capt. Fox, on the Island, and was organized by the appointment as temporary chairman, of Wm. S. Pierson, Esq., of Sandusky.

On nomination, the following appointments were made as officers of the day:

President of the Day—Gov. Salmon P. Chase, of Ohio.

Vice Presidents—Hon. Ross Wilkins, Detroit, Mich.; Judge H. V. Wilson, Cleveland, O.; Hon. E. Cooke, Sandusky, O.; Gen. John E. Hunt, Toledo, O.; Capt. Stephen Champlin, U. S. N., Buffalo; Maj. C. W. Hunter, Ill.; Hon. Joshua R. Giddings, Jefferson, O.; Hon. H. W. Baker, Norwalk, O.; Commander Joseph Lanman, U. S. N., Steamer Michigan; William B. Craighill, Esq., Pt. Clinton, O.

Secretaries—Geo. A. Benedict, Cleveland; H. D. Cooke, Sandusky; Wm. C. Earl, Toledo; J. A. Goodrich, Port Clinton; J. H. Herrick, Ravena; J. A. Harris, Cleveland; J. L. Newbury, Detroit.

Committee on Order of Exercises—B. Verner, Detroit, Mich.; Doct. McMeens, Sandusky, O.; H. V. Willson, Cleveland, O.; William Baker, Toledo, O.; Capt. Champlin, Buffalo, N. Y.; Lieut. Shirk, U. S. N.; Capt. H. A. Mitchell, U. S. Revenue Service.

Marshal of the Day—Gen. J. W. Fitch, Cleveland, O.

The Committee on Exercises reported the following:

National Salute by the U. S. Steamer Michigan.

Prayer by Rev. Dr. Duffield, of Philadelphia.

Introductory address by Gov. Chase.

Report from Wm. S. Pierson, Esq., of Sandusky, Chairman of Executive Committee of the Monument Association, on permanent organization.

The address of welcome to the officers and survivors of the war of 1813, by the Hon. E. Cooke of Sandusky.

Music, by White's Band, Toledo.

Response and address by Dr. Usher Parsons, the only known living survivor of the flag-ship Lawrence.

Song by Ossian E. Dodge, and the Barker family.

Address by Mayor Samuel Starkweather, of Cleveland.

Music, by Cleveland Band.

Ode by D. Bethune Duffield, Esq., of Detroit.

Music, by Yager Band, Sandusky.

Address by Judge Mason, Toledo.

Music, by the Independent Band, Detroit.

At 2 o'clock, a National Salute was fired by the U. S. Steamer Michigan, and the several Artillery companies on the ground.

The exercises followed in the order named in the programme. Gov. Chase opened the proceedings in a neat and elegant speech, as follows:

Fellow Citizens:—We are assembled to-day upon a most interesting occasion. Forty-five years ago this day, American valor met British valor, and American skill and conduct met British skill and conduct upon yonder Lake, and American valor, and skill, and conduct, triumphed—and may they ever triumph. [Applause.]

But we have met to-day to indulge in no feelings of exultation over a conquered foe; but to celebrate the greatness and the glory of our country, identified as they are and must be forever with the remembrance of the men by whom the triumph was achieved. We welcome here to-day the remnants of that gallant band who fought that battle. How delighted must be their eyes as they pass over scenes which meet them now—when they contrast that weakness with this strength, that comparatively feeble nation with this great and glorious people!

I said we have met together to interchange no feelings of exultation over the past, but to thank them who have achieved the inestimable blessings we enjoy, and rejoice that Providence has favored our prosperity. Why should we exult over that nation which was then our foe? Instead of meeting upon fields of battle, we are now peacefully engaged in commerce. Instead of answering cannon, and exchanging salutes upon fields of battle, our shouts of welcoming fly across the ocean and are re-echoed from thence across our mountains, until they lose themselves in the Pacific. Instead of sending our thoughts even by the slow methods of intercommunication, American perseverance and skill have traversed the ocean—not above it, but beneath—and lightning now speeds our words of cheer and welcome to our Anglo-Saxon brethren, while all our thoughts go up to Heaven in one expression, " God bless them."

We rejoice to welcome this vast multitude of citizens, to whom at last is to be conferred the destiny of the country. We rejoice to welcome the brave soldier, to whom our defence may be committed; the brave sailor, who defends the honor of his country; and last, but not least, we rejoice to welcome here to-day our fair country-women, by whom men are nurtured for the performance of the duties of life.

I am admonished, fellow-citizens, that we must be brief, for the sun will rapidly hasten to its setting. It has been thought that the best mode in which I could communicate it to the rest, will be to set the example. [Cheers.]

Gov. Chase's speech was enthusiastically received, and at its conclusion, W. S. Pierson, Esq., Chairman of the Monument Association, reported the following list of permanent officers of the association, which was adopted, viz.:

President—Hon. Lewis Cass, of Michigan.

Vice Presidents—Hon. Isaac Toucey, of Conn.; Dr. Usher Parsons, R. I.; Sidney Brooks, R. I.; Lieut. Thos. Brownell, U. S. N.; Gov.

Elisha Dyer, R. I.; Wm. Wetmore, Esq., R. I.; Hon. Edward Everett, Mass.; Hon. Wm. H. Seward, N. Y.; Auguste Belmont, Esq., N. Y.; Hon. Millard Fillmore, N. Y.; Capt. Stephen Champlin, N. Y.; Gov. W. F. Packer, Penn.; Wm. G. Moorehead, Esq., Penn.; Gov. S. P. Chase, Ohio; S. Starkweather, Cleveland; E. Cooke, Sandusky; S. L. Collins, Toledo; Ross Wilkins, Detroit; John Owen, Detroit; Col. Todd, Kentucky; Col. Jno. O'Fallan, St. Louis; J. Y. Scammer, Esq., Chicago; Hon. John Wentworth, Chicago; Capt. J. P. McKinstrey, U. S. N.; Commander Jos. Lanman, U. S. N.; Lt. Gen. Winfield Scott, U. S. Army.

On motion, Wm. S. Pierson, Esq., of Sandusky, was chosen Treasurer, and Dr. R. R. McMeens, of Sandusky, Corresponding Secretary.

COMMITTEE OF MANAGEMENT.

Sandusky—E. Cooke, Wm. S. Pierson, Pitt Cooke, O. Follett, A. H. Moss, Dr. R. R. McMeens, Jacob A. Camp, Dr. E. S. Lane, F. T. Barney, Geo. S. Patterson.

Cleveland—H. V. Willson, Geo. A. Benedict, J. W. Fitch, H. B. Payne, H. P. Weddell, M. Johnson, L. A. Pierce, J. P. Ross, John A. Foot, Samuel Starkweather.

Detroit—J. V. Campbell, E. C. Walker, H. B. Misner, G. V. N. Lathrop, S. D. Elwood, W. H. Craig, Ben. Verner, A. S. Williams, Jacob M. Howard, S. C. Andrews.

Toledo—Charles Kent, J. B. Steedman, C. B. Phillips, Peter Link, M. R. Waite, R. C. Lemmon, Robert H. Bill, S. J. Springer, Charles King, Perry Truax.

Buffalo—Capt. Stephen Champlin.

Fremont—Sardis Burchard.

Erie—W. W. Dobbins, Charles B. Wright, Charles M. Reed.

Port Clinton—John Jenney, J. H. Magruder.

Reviera St. Jago, New York; Capt. Lanman, U. S. Navy; Capt. Martin, Revenue Service; Capt. Ottinger, Revenue Service.

The following letters having been received were then read by the Chairman, W. S. Pierson :—

WASHINGTON CITY, Sept. 6th, 1858.

DEAR SIR:—Your invitation to me to form one of the numerous assemblage which will meet at Put-in-Bay on the 10th instant, has just been received, and while I thank you for remembering me in connection with that interesting occasion, I regret that it will be out of my power to avail myself of your kindness, as I shall be necessarily detained here by my public duties. But though absent I shall not the less participate in the feelings of gratitude and exultation, which the event you propose

14

to commemorate is so well calculated to inspire in every American breast. The Victory of Perry upon Lake Erie not far from the place of your convocation, on the 10th of September, 1813 was one of the most glorious, as well as one of the most important achievements recorded in our military annals.

I was with the Army then encamped in your region of country, during that hard fought contest, where we were all awaiting, with anxious solicitude, the operations of the fleet, as the command of the Lake was essential to our movements, and now after the elapse of almost half a century, it would rejoice me to hear my fellow citizens recall and recount the glories of that memorable day, mid the scenes where they were gained, and which they will ever illustrate. It is good for the American people to assemble together in the time of their strength to commemorate the deeds of patriotism and valor, which in the time of their weakness, enabled our country to pass safely through the trials, to which she was exposed. Such a tribute to departed worth is the object of the proposed convocation, and I beg leave to express my deep sympathy with the feelings which have prompted it.

With much regard, I am, dear Sir,

Truly yours,

LEWIS CASS.

Dr. R. R. McMeens.

Navy Department, Sept. 6th, 1858.

Dear Sir:—I have the honor to acknowledge the invitation, through you, of the Executive Committee to be present, on the 10th inst., at the inauguration and laying of the corner stone of a Monument to be erected on Gibraltar Rock, Put-in Bay Island, in commemoration of Perry's Victory.

I regret to state that my engagements will deprive me of the pleasure of participating with you on the interesting occasion.

I am with much respect,

Your obedient servant,

ISAAC TOUCEY.

R. R. McMeens, M. D.

Portsmouth, Va., Sept. 3d, 1858.

My Dear Sir:—I have received your esteemed favor of the 27th ult., requesting my presence and participation in the ceremonies at the contemplated inauguration of the Monument on Gibraltar Rock—in commemoration of our glorious naval triumph under the gallant Perry on the 10th September, 1813.

As one of the five surviving officers whose fortune it was, together with our brave tars, to be present on that glorious occasion, I thank you for your kind remembrance of me.

I regret that present indisposition precludes the pleasure of being with you to join you in doing honor to whom honor is so justly due,—the brave dead,—and renders imprudent at this time an absence from my home.

I am sir,   Your obedient servant,

H. N. PAGE.
Captain U. S. Navy.

R. R. McMeens, M. D.

Cincinnati, Sept, 9th, 1858.

Usher Parsons, M. D.

My Dear Doctor:—Yours of the 1st inst. arrived before my return from the " Yellow Springs," which afforded me no little pleasure to hear you intend to be at the glorious celebration at Put-in-Bay. I am denied the pleasure of participating with you in consequence of sickness. I confidently flattered myself 12 days ago, I would be enabled to be present and unite with the few survivors in celebrating the most brilliant achievement of the memorable battle of Lake Erie, on the 10th September, 1813, in which battle I was. Shortly after Col. Crogan's Victory where I was on the morning after the British made good their retreat, I volunteered at Camp Seneca, and was led by Gen. Wm. Henry Harrison to Perry's fleet.

I pray the good people who have been instrumental in promoting the celebration may continue it annually for all time to come.

May the blessing of Heaven guide and preserve all who attend the celebration, truly and sincerely is my prayer.

Most sincerely your friend,

W. T. TALIAFERRO.

New York, August 28th, 1858.

Mr F. T. Barney, Sandusky City, O. :

My Dear Sir:—In answer to your favor

of the 21st inst. on the subject of the erection of a monument on the little Island of Gibraltar, I have to say: that if *said Monument be to the memory of Commodore Perry*, as I *suppose* it is, I will be too happy to contribute to it, not only by the free gift of the land requisite, but by procuring subscriptions in New York and one or two other places, which I think I can do; I accordingly hereby confer upon you and my friend Simon Fox, power to grant a sufficient part of the said Island of Gibraltar, in perpetuity, for the erection of said monument, with such reservations as you may deem necessary to prevent any sort of injury to my property in the group of Islands. It would please me if I and my successors after me, were appointed keepers of the ground ceded, and of the monument.

Respectfully yours,

RIVERA St. JAGO.

———

After the adoption of the above organization, and the reading of letters, Gov. Chase introduced Hon. E. Cooke, of Sandusky, who spoke as follows:

Ladies, Gentlemen, Fellow Countrymen:

I rise, as the organ of the Executive Committee, to bid you welcome to these classic shores, immortalized by American valor and rich in the associations of a nation's glory. But how can I find language suitably to express my congratulations to the assembled thousands who surround me, and whose presence this day, gives the lie to the reproach that " Republics know not how to be grateful." If I could hope to be heard, by an audience so immense, I would thank you in the name of our Common Country, for having come up in such vast numbers from the beautiful cities of the Lake and the interior, to this patriotic consecration. But with a voice, impaired by the wasting power of many years, I can hope to say but litttle else, than to offer up my fervent thanksgiving to Almighty God, for those evidences of enthusiastic gratitude and patriotic devotion, which the occasion has inspired, and which your presence this day proclaims.

We have met to commemorate one of those rare and signal events, which, considering the vast interests it involved, the glory it achieved and the benefits conferred, has few parallels in history. We shall find it difficult, however, justly to appreciate the importance of Perry's Victory, without calling to mind, for a moment, the peculiar condition of our country which preceded and followed its achievements. A sanguinary war had for more than a year been raging between Great Britain and the United States. How it was sustained on the land and on the ocean, history has recorded. It must be admitted, however, that its commencement on the Niagara and in the Northwest, was characterized by defeat, disaster and disgrace. Whether the inglorious surrender of the fortress of Detroit and the consequent uncontrolled possession of the vast Northwestern Territory by the enemy, was chargeable to treachery or cowardice, it is not now necessary to inquire. The event smote the heart of the nation with dismay and covered the whole land with conscious humiliation. Our whole vast frontier from Buffalo to Arkansas, was at once thrown open to the stroke of the tomahawk, and exposed bare and defenceless to the merciless incursions of the savage foe. The authority and protection of the United States had ceased within its borders. The course of the enemy, leagued with their savage allies, was everywhere marked with rapine, massacre and devastation. The heart-rending and bloody tragedy of the River Rasin — and other doomed localities, followed in succession. Consternation and alarm everywhere prevailed. Thousands "without distinction of age or sex" were expelled from their peaceful abodes by the invading foe, and the face of Heaven was insulted by the murder of men, women and children, and by the wanton conflagration of defenceless cabins and villages. The flower and chivalry of the land were cut off in their glory, and their bones whitened the face of the wilderness. Deeds of cruelty and unutterable horror were enacted, which filled the whole land with lamentation and wrung drops of agony from the heart of the nation. A dark cloud hung over our devoted country, throwing down from its frowning armory the paleness of death upon her cheek, and its coldnesss upon her bosom. True, the assaults upon the defences of Harrison and Croghan, on the Maumee and Sandusky, had been gallantly and gloriously repelled. But these exploits, brilliant as they were, availed little to the relief of the frontiers, while the entire possession of the lake by a well manned fleet of Veterans, remained in the undisputed control of the foe, with power to descend, at any moment, with their combined forces, upon any portion of our exposed frontier. The crisis demanded *action, vigorous action,* combined with valor and talent to direct it. The *command of the Lake had become to us* INDISPENSIBLE. In view of this, the creation of an American fleet, the timber for which was then growing in the wilderness, was ordered by our Government, as well for purposes of protection as invasion. In March, 1813, the charge of its construction and command, was assigned to Oliver H. Perry, of Rhode Island, who in spite of almost superhuman obstacles and difficulties, in less than three months completed his work and launched his vessels at the harbor of Erie. But although he frequently sought to engage the enemy, he was unable to bring them into action, until the ever memorable and ever glorious day we have met to commemorate.

Of the battle and its thrilling incidents, I have no time to speak. I am not here, with a tongue of fire, to relight and emblazon the splendors of the achievement. That office must be left for a more elaborate address, and to others better fitted for the task. And I rejoice to say that some of its touching details will be given you to-day, in burning words, from a living and honored actor in the scene. On this point, therefore, I need only add, that although between single ships on the ocean, the trial had been before signally glorious to our flag, yet *this* was the first American Squadron that ever made battle with an enemy, and this "was the first English fleet, since England had a navy, that ever had been captured." And if anything further were wanting to heighten the brilliancy of the achievement, it may be found in the fact that *our* fleet was inadequately and unequally provided with men and cannon,—manned mostly by raw recruits, uninured to battle, and commanded by *young men*, without experience in naval warfare! While on the other hand that of the British was fully armed—furnished with men who had encountered many conflicts on the ocean, and commanded by the experienced and veteran Commander Barclay, who had won rich laurels under Nelson, at the immortal Battle of Trafalgar! !

Such was the tremendous contrast between the opposing forces! shut now the volume that records the event, and tell me, thou man of naval or military science, upon what principle of human probability can the triumph of our arms, in a conflict so unequal, be predicted?

The contrast was great, but, to the dauntless Perry, by no means appalling. After the line of battle had been set, and all was made ready, —an hour—a silent hour was occupied in advancing to the conflict:—an hour, in which the lives of the squadron, the fate of the North-west, and the honor of the nation were suspended upon the talents and collected valor of *one man!* How appalling the responsibility! How terrible the probation! How vast the interests involved! How intense the gaze of millions upon the issue! At such a moment, men of the present generation, picture to yourselves the solemn spectacle, the sublime pageantry of two hostile armies, watching the movement from the opposite shores of the Lake—of defenceless thousands throughout the unprotected regions of the North-west, whose lives and homes were at stake; yea, of the millions of two great nations, whose *final* triumph hung upon the issue—all, all awaiting with breathless anxiety the result of the conflict, and tell me if it was not an hour in which the stoutest heart of the Hero charged with such a battle might have justly trembled? Yet, the heroic Perry remained unagitated, unshaken and invincible! He had no fear, but for the safety and honor of his country: no ambition, but to conquer or die in her defence.

At a quarter before 12 o'clock, the solemn suspense was broken, and the conflict began. At 3 o'clock the battle ended. Its thunders were hushed. Their echoes had died away upon the distant shores of the lake, and the deep "silence of nature" succeeded, broken only by the cries of the wounded and the dying."........ As the smoke of Battle rolled away, it revealed a victory, which shed undying glory upon the Republic, and gave immortal renown to the victors......... A victory which wiped from our escutcheon the disgrace of Hull's surrender, avenged the insulted honor of our flag, and dissolved forever the spell of boasted British maritime invincibility. THE PUPIL OF NELSON HAD struck to the youthful Perry, and the country rang with acclamations of joy!

In estimating the immediate and momentous results of this victory, it should not be forgotten that it at once opened a pathway for Gen. Harrison, to the subjugation of Fort Malden, to, the re-conquest of Detroit,—to the restoration of peace and safety to our whole extended frontier, and to the crowning glory of his campaign, by the capture of the entire British army, at the Battle of the Thames ! It changed at once the entire theatre of the war in this region, and transferred it, with all its dread pageantry of death and devastation from our own soil,— to that of the bewildered and astonished and panic-stricken foe. And, it is no exaggeration to assert that from the moment of this victory, the ambitious schemes of the enemy upon our western borders were forever blasted, and that the last vestige of British domination in the Northwest practically expired with the expiring notes of the last cannon, whose thunders closed the battle of Lake Erie !

In view of these grand and glorious results—connected with the direct influence they exerted—to revive the public spirit, to restore fresh vigor to the American arms:—to waken the national confidence:—to sustain the national credit and to strengthen the arms of the Government, at that gloomy period of the war, it is no wonder that the news of the victory flew on the wings of the wind, electrifying the whole nation with joy and filling the heart of every patriot with gratitude and exultation ! No wonder that the bells of every church throughout the Republic, rang out their merry peals as the news traversed the interior, and that every city and hamlet in the land blazed forth with bonfires and illuminations and other manifestations of the highwrought public rejoicings.

And shall we, who are now in the peaceful enjoyment of the full fruition of these results:—shall *we*, standing here in sight of the spot where the great battle which secured them was fought and won:—shall WE, who have fixed our homes and set up our household gods in the midst of the Territory thus rescued and defended—remain indifferent to an event which conferred such priceless blessings, which cost so much blood and peril to achieve it, which added so much wealth to the fame of the nation, and which still commands the applause and admiration of the world? No, never, never.

To these scenes, then, let us with each returning anniversary come up for our instruction. Let us here re-kindle the beacon-fires of patriotism, which Perry left, on yonder cliff, with a fervent prayer that they might *burn forever*. Let us bring honors this day for the noble dead who perished in the fight—and let the laurel and the cypress be kept forever fresh and green upon the lonely graves where their ashes are enshrined. In a word, let us seek our great practical lessons of public duty and patriotic daring in the contemplation of the exploits and sacrifices of that dauntless band, who near this spot, perilled their lives for their country. But above all, let us this day signalize our grateful appreciation of their glorious deeds, by efficient measures for the erection of a monument on yonder " Gibraltar Rock," to the memory of Perry and his noble companions,—there to stand forever, a perpetual memorial of our convictions of the unmeasured benefits conferred upon the Western States by their patriotic and heroic valor.

At no distant day, upon that consecrated spot where sleep the ashes of the brave, who fell in the conflict; "with solemnities suited to the occasion; with prayers to Almighty God for his blessing," and in the midst of a cloud of witnesses like those which surround me,—let the corner stone of that Monument be laid. There, let it rise:—there let it stand as long as the blue waters of Erie shall continue to dash against its rock-bound base, to mark the spot, which must be forever dear to us, to our children, and to our children's children, down to the latest syllable of recorded time.

The lapse of forty-five years has laid down in the dust most of the brave men who participated in the victory. The illustrious chief himself, who on that proud day, amid the roar and smoke and storm of battle, inscribed his name upon the shield of immortality, has been compelled to yield to the only foe he could not conquer; but all, thank Heaven, are not yet gone. A little remnant of that immortal band still linger among the living, to reap the rich rewards of their labors and perils, in the affections and benedictions of their countrymen:—and four of these have kindly yielded to the earnest invitations of the Committee, and are now present, to receive an expression of the gratitude of the country, for which they put their lives at hazard, and to which they devoted the flower of their youth.

Fortunate should we esteem ourselves that we have been permitted to behold this spectacle: a spectacle, the like of which in thrilling interest and imposing grandeur, was never before vouchsafed to the present generation. Happy, indeed, that God has granted us the sight of these veteran survivors, under circumstances so novel and affecting. Soon, alas! too soon, shall we seek in vain for *one* survivor, and the last of the heroic band will be seen on earth no more forever. Let us then bring fresh honors, this day, to those who still remain to link the living with the dead, ere the grave shall have closed upon them forever.

Gallant and venerable men! With grateful hearts we bid you welcome, thrice welcome, to these Island shores, and to these bright scenes of your early glory. We thank the God of Mercy for having prolonged your lives, that we might thus greet *you*, and that *you* might behold this deeply earnest demonstration of your grateful countrymen.

On revisiting the memorable spot where you linked forever your own fame with the glory of your country, after the absence of nearly half a century, it is not strange that the stirring incidents of the victory, in which you so honorably shared, should come down upon your memory, like an avalanche from the past, and agitate you with conflicting emotions.

How changed the scene, since your eyes last beheld these lovely shores! True, the same lake which you then saw wreathed in the smoke of battle and encrimsoned with the blood of your companions—still continues its ceaseless funereal wail over the slumbers of the buried brave, or chants its loud anthems to the praise of your gallant deeds. The same sun, which then looked down from his mid-day throne, and fired your young hearts to deeds of glorious daring, still smiles upon your return to this renowned theatre of your youthful courage and patriotism. But in other respects how great the change! The haughty foe is gone —the din of war is hushed, and instead of the thunders of hostile cannon and the shrieks of your dying comrades, you have heard to-day the shouts of a *new* generation, who have come out from all the borders of the lovely land you defended, to greet you with the loud acclaim of an overflowing and universal gratitude.

Forever hereafter the 10th of September, 1813, shall be as sacred to our hearts, as it has long been glorious to our annals. It was your good fortune, most honorably, to participate in the dangers of that day. Imminent were the perils you encountered; glorious the deeds you performed, and great the sacrifices you made for your country. I will not attempt their eulogy. They have already found their place with those of your departed compatriots, among the solemn archives of our country, where they can never die:—and the history which records them is but an imperishable transcript of your claims upon our gratitude.

You have come to most of the thousands before you as from a distant age, to revive recollections and recount incidents, around which the mists of tradition had began to cluster: and you find yourselves to-day in the midst of a generation, now in the full vigor and meridian strength of manhood, who had not seen the light of Heaven, when you here nobly bared your breasts to the shafts of death, in defence of the rights and honor of your country.

You are now, where you stood forty-five years ago, with trailed banners at the burial of your valiant dead. Like myself, you belong to a former generation. You look around you in vain for your youthful companions in arms and brothers in peril. They have been gathered to their fathers. But you look around you not in vain for the evidences of your country's happiness, and for the rich rewards of your patriotic sacrifices and toils:—you look around you not in vain for the joy and gratitude of the living thousands who surround you, and who have been made happy — *most happy* — to bid you welcome, thrice welcome, on this consecrated day.

We forbear further to betray our emotions: for eulogy belongs less to the living than to the dead: and there is not a heart, throughout this vast assembly, that does not fervently pray that we may long be spared the duty of granting to you our last and highest honors. Distant, far distant be the day which shall mark your setting sun. May the same God who shielded you in battle, and guided and preserved you in after life, still smile upon your declining years, and cover them with his richest and choicest blessings.

After the applause which followed the close of this address had subsided, Mr. Cooke introduced to the audience Capt. Stephen Champlin, as the last surviving commander of the Perry Squadron, who led the Scorpion in the front line of the battle, and who fired the *first* and *last* gun in the conflict. He was received with tremendous cheers. Whereupon Gov. Chase read the following highly appropriate response, in lieu of a speech, from the modest but gallant commander:—

MR. PRESIDENT:—Unaccustomed to speak in public, and having no confidence in my voice, I ask the favor of you to read the following reply to the flattering sentiments just offered:

FELLOW CITIZENS:—I cordially thank you, for the distinguished honors paid to the memory of my old commander, Commodore O. H. Perry, and the gallant officers and men under his command in the battle on this lake—and also the flattering notice of my services on that occasion,

—you have hereby amply rewarded me for the toil and exposure of life on that eventful day—next to a consciousness that I performed my duty faithfully is the approbation of so vast a multitude of my fellow citizens: I renewedly thank you, and beg leave to offer the following sentiment:

" The thirty-six volunteers of General Harrison's Army, who came to our assistance in our greatest need, to whom we were much indebted for their valuable services."

Six rousing cheers were here given for Capt. Champlin.

Mr. Cooke next introduced the venerable William Blair, of Lexington, Richland county, Ohio—as one of the thirty-six volunteers of Gen. Harrison's army just referred to—and exhibited to the audience from the neck of the old veteran, a rich and massive silver medal, bearing the impress of Perry, with appropriate inscriptions—which had been voted to him, with the thanks of the Commonwealth by the State of Pennsylvania, of which he was then a citizen, in testimony of his patriotism and bravery at the battle of Lake Erie. The old hero was too much affected to say one word, but amidst a storm of applause acknowledged the kindness shown him, by a modest bow and a flood of tears.

Mr. Cooke then introduced Lieut. Thomas Brownell, of Newport, R. I., who was second in command of the schooner Ariel. The appearance of this brave and faithful officer, was greeted with overwhelming applause. He responded by thanking his fellow-citizens for this flattering and cordial expression of their feelings, and assured them that it was gratefully appreciated by him.

Dr. Usher Parsons, of Providence, R. I., the surgeon of the flag-ship Lawrence, at the time of the battle, was then introduced and gave a detailed and thrilling account of the engagement. His address was listened to with the most intense interest, and was frequently interrupted with cheers that made the welkin ring. The following is the address entire :

Mr. President and Citizens of the Lake Shore :

The survivors of the battle of Lake Erie here present, have listened with intense interest to the eloquent address just delivered, and thank you most sincerely for the cordial reception you have given to its friendly and complimentary allusions to our services on the day we are now assembled to commemorate.

Forty-five years ago, we were here as spectators and participators in the battle, and now, in advanced years, are invited to join a vast number of patriotic citizens, gathered from the beautiful and flourishing cities bordering this Lake, to celebrate the victory then gained by our squadron.

We have come hither, my friends, to honor the memory of those who fell in that glorious conflict, and are sleeping under the soil near where we are now gathered. We have come also to pay a grateful tribute of respect to the memory of Commodore Perry and his associates in the battle, who have since passed away in the ordinary course of human life. And you, citizens of the Lake shore, have sought out and invited here a little remnant of survivors to bless our eyes with the evidences of your prosperity and happiness, and to warm our hearts with tokens of assurance that our toils and peril of life on that eventful day are not forgotten. Would to God that more had been spared to participate with us in these generous demonstrations of gratitude and respect. But they have passed away; and in a very brief period of time, no spectator will be left to tell the story of Perry's Victory.

That victory derives a general interest, from the fact that it was the first encounter of our infant navy, in fleet or squadron. In combats with single ships, we had humbled the pride of Great Britain. The Guerrier, Java, and Macedonia, had surrendered to our stars and stripes. But here, on yonder waves, that nation was taught the unexpected lesson that we could conquer them in squadron. But this battle derives a particular interest from its bearing on the war of 1812, and from the relief it brought to your shores;—in wresting the tomahawk and scalping knife from savage hands;—shielding a frontier of three hundred miles, from assaults and conflagrations of a combined British and savage foe;—opening the gates of Malden to General Harrison's army, that enabled it to pursue and capture the only army that was captured during the war; and in restoring to us Detroit, and the free navigation of the upper Lakes.

My friends, you have read, and your fathers have told you the story of this victory. Yet, from the interest you still manifest by coming here in thronging multitudes, as well as by the expressed wish of some present and of the press, it is apparent that you wish the story to be repeated, probably with the desire that you may hereafter relate it to your children, as coming from a spectator of the scene: I will, therefore, give a brief sketch of the battle:

I shall not detain you with a history of the construction and equipment of the squadron, and of the many difficulties encountered, but commence with our arrival here twenty-five days before the action, and our cruising in that time between Malden and Sandusky, and receiving near the latter place, a visit from Gen. Harrison and suite, preparatory to an attack on Malden.

Early in the morning of the 10th of September, 1813, while we lay at anchor in this Bay, a cry came from mast-head—"sail! ho!" all hands leaped from their berths, and in a few minutes the cry was repeated, until six sail were announced. Signal was made to the squadron—"*Enemy in sight! get under way!*" and soon the hoarse sound of trumpets and shrill pipe of the boatswains resounded throughout our squadron with "*all hands up anchor ahoy!*"

In passing out of this Bay, it was desirable to go to the left of yonder islet, but on being notified by Sailing Master Taylor that adverse winds would prevent, the Commodore replied, go then sir to the right, for this day I am determined to meet and fight the enemy.

There were nine American vessels, carrying 54 guns and 400 men, and six British vessels carrying 63 guns and 511 men.

At the head of our line were the Scorpion, Capt. Champlin, and Ariel, Lieut. Packet—next the flag-ship Lawrence, of 20 guns, to engage the flag-ship Detroit, the Caledonia to fight the Hunter; the Niagara of 20 guns, to engage the Queen Charlotte, and lastly, three small vessels to fight the Lady Provost, of 13 guns, and Little Belt, of 3 guns. Our fleet moved on to attack the enemy, distant at 10 o'clock, about five miles. The Commodore now produced the *Burgee*, or fighting flag, hitherto concealed in the ship. It was inscribed with large white letters on a blue ground, legible throughout the squadron—"*Don't give up the Ship*"—the last words of the expiring Lawrence, and now to be hoisted at the mast-head of the vessel bearing his name. A spirited appeal was made to the crew, and up went the flag to the fore-royal, amid hearty cheers repeated throughout the squadron—and the drums and fifes struck up the thrilling sound—*all hands to quarters.* The hatches or passage-way to the deck were now closed, excepting a small aperture ten inches square, through which light was admitted into the Surgeon's room, for receiving the wounded, the floor of which was on a level with the surface of the Lake, and exposing them to cannon balls as much as if they were on deck.

Every preparation being made, and every man at his station, a profound silence reigned more than an hour, the most trying part of the scene. It was like the stillness that precedes the hurricane. The fleet moved on steadily till a quarter before 12, when the awful suspense was relieved by a shot aimed at us from the Detroit, about one mile distant. Perry made more sail, and coming within canister distance, opened a rapid and destructive fire upon the Detroit. The Caledonia, Capt. Turner, followed the Lawrence in gallant style, and the Ariel, Lieut. Packet, and the Scorpion, Mr. Champlin, fought nobly and effectively.

The Niagara failing to grapple with the Queen, the latter vessel shot ahead to fire upon the Lawrence, and with the Detroit, aimed their broadsides exclusively upon her, hoping and intending to sink her. At last they made her a complete wreck, but, fortunately the Commodore escaped without injury, and stepping into a boat with his fighting flag thrown over his shoulder, he pushed off for the Niagara amid a shower of cannon and musket balls, and reached that vessel unscathed. He found her a fresh vessel, with only two, or at most, three persons injured, and immediately sent her commander to hasten up the small vessels. Perry boarded the Niagara when she was abreast of the Lawrence, and further from her than the Detroit was on her right. The Lawrence now dropt astern and hauled down her flag. Perry turned the Niagara's course toward the enemy, and crossing the bows of the Lawrence, bore down headforemost to the enemy's line, determined to break through it and take a raking position. The Detroit attempted to turn, so as to keep her broadside to the Niagara, and avoid being raked, but in doing this, she fell against the Queen, and got entangled n her rigging, which left the enemy no alternative but to strike both ships. Perry now shot further ahead near the Lady Provost, which, from being crippled in her rudder, had drifted out of her place to the leeward, and was pressing forward toward the head of the British line to support the two ships. One broadside from the Niagara silenced her battery. The Hunter next struck, and the two smaller vessels in attempting to escape, were overhauled by the Scorpion, Mr. Champlin, and Trip, Mr. Holdup, and thus ended the action, after 3 o'clock.

Let us now advert for a moment to the scenes exhibited in the flag-ship Lawrence, of which I can speak as an eye-witness. The wounded began to come down before she opened her battery, and for one, I felt impatient at the delay. In proper time, however, as it proved, the dogs of war were let loose from their leash, and it seemed as though heaven and earth were at loggerheads. For more than two hours, little could be heard but the deafening thunders of our broadsides, the crash of balls dashing through our timbers, and the shrieks of the wounded. These were brought down faster than I could attend to them, farther than to stay the bleeding, or support a shattered limb with splints, and pass them forward upon the berth-deck.

When the battle had raged an hour and a half, I heard a call for me at the small sky-light, and stepping toward it, I saw the Commodore, whose countenance was as calm and as placid, as if on ordinary duty. "Doctor," said he, "send me one of your men," meaning one of the six stationed with me to assist in moving the wounded. In five minutes the call was repeated and obeyed, and at the seventh call, I told him he had all my men. He asked if there were any sick or wounded who could pull a rope, when two or three crawled upon deck to lend a feeble hand in pulling at the last guns.

The hard fighting terminated about 3 o'clock. As the smoke cleared away, the two fleets were found mingled together, the small vessels having come up to the others. The shattered Lawrence lying to the windward, was once more able to hoist her flag, which was cheered by a few feeble voices on board, making a melancholy sound compared with the boisterous cheers that preceded the battle.

The proud, though painful duty of taking possession of the conquered ships, was now performed. The Detroit was nearly dismantled, and the destruction and carnage had been dreadful. The Queen was in a condition little better—every commander, and second in command, says Barclay in his official report, was either killed or wounded. The whole number killed in the British fleet, was forty-one, and of wounded, ninety-four. In the American fleet, twenty-seven killed, and ninety-six wounded. Of the twenty-seven killed, twenty-two were on board the Lawrence, and of the ninety-six wounded, sixty-one were on board this same ship, making 83 killed and wounded out of 101 reported fit for duty in the Lawrence on the morning of the battle. On board the Niagara were two killed, and twenty-three wounded, making twenty-five, and of these, twenty-two were killed or wounded after Perry took command of her.

About four o'clock a boat was discovered approaching the Lawrence. Soon the commodore was recognized in her, who was returning to resume the command of his tattered ship, determined that the remnant of her crew should have the privilege of witnessing the formal surrender of the British officers. It was a time of conflicting emotions when he stepped upon the deck. The battle was won, and he was safe, but the deck was slippery with blood, and strewed with the bodies of twenty officers and men, some of whom sat at table with us at our last meal, and the ship resounded with the groans of the wounded. Those of us who were spared and able to walk, met him at the gangway to welcome him on board, but the salutation was a silent one on both sides—not a word could find utterance. And now the British officers arrived, one from each vessel, to tender their submission, and with it their swords. When they approached, picking their way among the wreck and carnage of the deck with their hilts toward Perry, they tendered them to his acceptance. With a dignified and solemn air, and with a low tone of voice, he requested them to retain their side arms, inquired with deep concern for Commodore Barclay and the wounded officers, tendering to them every comfort his ship afforded, and expressing his regret that he had not a spare medical officer to send them, that he only had one on duty for the fleet, and that one had his hands full.

Among the ninety-six wounded there occurred three deaths; a result so favorable was attributable to the plentiful supply of fresh provisions sent off to us from the Ohio shore; to fresh air,—the wounded being ranged under an awning on the deck until we arrived at Erie, ten days after the action, and also to the devoted attention of Commodore Perry to every want.

Those who were killed in the battle were that evening committed to the deep, and over them was read the impressive Episcopal service.

On the following morning the two fleets sailed into this bay, where the slain officers of both were buried in an appropriate and affecting manner. They consisted of three Americans, Lieutenant Brooks and midshipmen Laub and Clarke, and three British Officers, Captain Finnis and Lieut. Stokes of the Queen, and Lieutenant Garland, of the Detroit. Equal respect was paid to the slain of both nations, and the crews of both fleets united in the ceremony. The procession of boats, with two bands of music—the slow and regular motion of the oars, striking in exact time with the notes of the solemn dirge, the mournful waving of flags and sound of minute guns from the ships, presented a striking contrast to the scene presented two days before, when both the living and the dead, now forming in this solemn and fraternal train, were engaged in fierce and bloody strife, hurling at each other the thunderbolts of war.

On the eighth day after the action, the Lawrence was dispatched to Erie with the wounded, where we received a cordial welcome and kind hospitality. The remainder of the vessels conveyed Harrison's army to to Malden, where they found the public stores in flames, and Proctor with his army in hasty retreat. Perry joined Harrison as a volunteer aid, who with our troops, chiefly from Ohio and Kentucky, overtook and captured the army. Perry then accompanied Harrison and Commodore Barclay to Erie, where they landed amid peals of cannon and and shouts of the multitude, and from thence he proceeded to Rhode Island.

Commodore Perry served two years as commander of the Java, taking with him most of the survivors of the Lawrence. He after this commanded a squadron in the West Indies, where he died in 1819.

Possessed of high-toned morals, he was above the low dissipation and sensuality too prevalent with some officers of his day, and in his domestic character was a model of every domestic virtue and grace. His literary acquirements were respectable, and his taste refined. He united the graces of a manly beauty to a lion heart, a sound mind, a safe judgment, and a firmness of purpose which nothing could shake.

But this intelligent audience already know and appreciate his noble virtues and honor his glorious achievements. The maps of your shores and inland towns and counties are inscribed with his name; and the noble State of Ohio and the United States, are about to decorate the walls of their respective capitols with splendid representations of the battle we are this day commemorating.

My friends, in the name and behalf of the citizens of Rhode Island, I tender you their grateful acknowledgments for the honor done that little State on this interesting occasion. She sent hither the Commander of the squadron, and a majority of the officers and men. She glories in the victory gained, and regards the name and fame of her gallant son as one of her choicest jewels, and will ever cherish grateful sentiments towards those who respect and honor his memory. You have come hither, my friends, for this holy purpose from all the cities of the lake shores, and are about to lay the corner stone to a monument to perpetuate his memory and fame. Though his name will outlive structures of marble or of bronze, yet rest asured that the citizens of Rhode Island will hail with delight the report of this day's transactions, and in their future western pilgrimages will linger about this spot and invoke Heaven's choicest blessings on you in return for your generous magnanimity.

Old companions in the conflict, I rejoice to see you and once more take you by the hand, and a more fitting occasion than the present could hardly occur or be conceived of. In the days of our youth we came to the rescue of this Lake, and to assist in restoring peace to the frontier. A kind Providence has lengthened out our days beyond man's allotted period of existence, and now, after the lapse of nearly half a century, permits us to revisit the place where important scenes transpired in our early years, and to unite in celebrating the victory achieved by our much loved commander. We joyfully survey the wonderful changes and improvements that have occurred since the war of 1812. Buffalo was then a populous village, but soon after a heap of ashes. Erie contained but a score of dwellings. Cleveland was a cluster of log cabins, Sandusky the same, Toledo was nowhere, and Detroit in possession of the enemy; and not a single American vessel was left on the lakes, on which to hoist our stars and stripes.

And what do we behold now? A population increased an hundred fold; magnificent and prosperous cities, lofty spires and domes on temples of worship; colleges and seminaries of learning; extensive commerce; railroads diverging and intersecting in all directions; the white outspread wings of commerce gliding to and fro, and freighted with the exhaustless products of the North and North-west,—aye, and ploughing yon crystal waves, once shrouded in the smoke of our cannon, and crimsoned with the blood of our companions.

Old friends, we part to day, probably to meet no more. Our memories of the past, and the happy experiences of this celebration, fill our hearts with grateful and tender emotions, and will serve to gild the evening twilight of our days. I bid you an affectionate farewell.

At the conclusion of Dr. Parson's address, a patriotic song, prepared for the occasion, was sung by Ossian E. Dodge and the Barker Family.*

Mayor Starkweather, of Cleveland, was then announced, and addressed the assemblage in the following spirited and patriotic speech:

Mr. Starkweather in speaking for the large company, of the citizens of Cleveland, who had come to honor this occasion by their presence, said, that if it was possible for them to feel a greater interest in it than some others, it was because the fate of that city, for the time, was involved in the issue of the battle we have met to commemorate.

Mr. S. spoke of the feelings with which the whole population of their then infant city, rushed to the water's side when aroused by the distant thunders of that great battle, and of the painful suspense with which they listened to the echoes, which might be tidings of its results, and how exultant they became of our victory, when they heard the big guns fired the last; for however, in argument, said Mr. S., they may not succeed who have the last words, in battle they are sure of the victory who fire the last guns, and we have the pleasure of now seeing upon the stand, the heroic Champlin, by whose order they were fired to arrest a captive ship in its attempt to escape.

Forty five years, said Mr. S., have now passed away, since our gallant men, who fell in that battle, have been reposing beneath yonder willow in their lonely graves, and now after the lapse of so many years, we have the satisfaction to behold this vast multitude, who have come to honor these graves, and who have come resolving with one heart, that upon this sacred spot a monument shall arise, commemorative of the great battle of Lake Erie, and worthy of the heroes who achieved our glorious victory.

To estimate the importance of that battle, we have only to know that upon its results depended the safety of our whole frontier from the Straits of Macinac to the Falls of Niagara, and what was more than all,

*See Incidents of the Day.

upon its results depended the honor of the American navy, and that to
conceive of the sensations occasioned by its results, we must realize that
between two of the most powerful, most Christian and kindred nations
of the earth, there was a deadly war, that here was the dividing line
of their dominions, that across this water each must pass, in the attempt
to invade the territory of the other, and that here was destined to be felt
their great encounter for supremacy on this inland sea. And here Mr. S.
proceeded to describe at some length the scenes presented on the eve of
the battle, the belligerent armies of Harrison and Proctor, as they stood
upon those opposite shores, waiting the result, and the opposing fleets as
they approached each other, and it was there, said Mr. S., by yonder
beautiful island called " Western Sister, " they met, and what a meeting
was there ? England had until then, been the proud mistress of the
seas. " Brittiania rules the waves " had been the theme and the sentiment of her national songs. Upon this element she claimed to be invincible, and though under the stars and stripes, the charm of her invincibility had been broken, it was in a conflict of ship with ship, but it
was now to be tested in a conflict of fleet with fleet.

When the brave Perry led his gallant men into that fierce, unequal,
and for a time that doubtful conflict, well may he be supposed to have
addressed them in the language like that of the renowned Henry the 5th
on the eve of the battle of Agincourt, when he is thus made to speak :

> " He that outlives this day, and comes safe home,
> Will stand a tip-toe when this day is named.
> He that shall live this day, and see old age,
> Will yearly on the vigil feast his friends,
> And say—to-morrow is St. Crispian.
> Old men forget; yet all shall be forgot;
> But he'll remember, with advantages,
> What feats he did this day; then shall our names
> Familiar in their mouths as household words,
> Be in their flowing cups freshly remembered."

And forever memorable in American annals, will be the day we celebrate, and upon each return of this day, multitudes in happy throngs,
will come to visit this sacred spot, to look upon this land and this water,
once the scenes of such memorable events, and that they may behold
its change, from a scene of bloody strife, to scenes of the most happy
intercourse, and rejoice in the contemplation that the nations which
warred against each other here, have forgotten all their animosities,
will war against each other no more, and that to unite the hearts of these
two great nations, a chord has been laid across the great ocean, and
slender and delicate as was that chord, it would never be broken, for it
has been laid under the favoring dispensation of Heaven, and under its
edict " whom God hath joined together, let no man put asunder."

In response to a general call from the multitude, Hon. Joshua R. Giddings was then introduced by Gov. Chase. He said that the scenes of the conflict of 1813 were familiar to him. Forty-six years ago he was a soldier, bearing knapsack and blanket. In breathless silence all awaited the result of this famous battle. For three long hours they listened to the booming of the cannon. Long before they had got any correct information it was said we had achieved a victory. It was an awful day—that Tenth of September. May God spare you from witnessing scenes to which our veteran friends here were so familiar. Why should men, worshipping the same God and trusting in the same salvation, slay each other? Perry stood for the maintenance of high and holy principles of right—the right of man to enjoy liberty and develop his moral nature. The battle for right is still raging. But a hundred men will fly in civil life where one will yield on the battle-field. To you is committed the maintenance of the rights for which our friends fought and bled—they have done their duty, will you do yours? May you prove worthy of all the blessings which have been conferred upon you!

An ode prepared for the occasion by D. Bethune Duffield, Esq., of Detroit, was next announced by the President of the day, who made a playful allusion to the infancy of Michigan at the time of the battle. This called out the Hon. Ross Wilkins, of Detroit, who rejoined in a humorous and telling speech. Michigan, he said, though an infant at that time, was now full grown, and one of the fairest of the sisterhood of States. She asked no odds of Ohio, because the latter happened to be a few years the elder of the two. But she *would* defer to the claims of Rhode Island—"little Rhody"—who was so well represented here to-day, and whose gallant sons so well maintained the national honor, on this same field forty-five years ago. "Indeed," said Judge Wilkins, the battle of Lake Erie was a *Rhode Island fight.* Her sons were the most conspicuous participants in the hazards and glories of the engagement. Immortal honor was stamped upon her proud escutcheon by the gallant acts of her brave sons on that memorable occasion. While Michigan was ready to concede to her sister States every thing that is their due, she will yet stand up for her rights. The speaker humorously referred to the squabble, commonly known as the "Toledo War," between Michigan and Ohio, over a piece of territory, in which contest his State came out behind. But she would some day make up for this defeat, if possible.

The speaker then introduced D. Bethune Duffield, Esq., who delivered the following poem of felicitous conception, patriotic sentiment, and rare beauty and finish. It is an admirable effort, worthy our most pretentious poets, and was pronounced by the Survivors present "the most accurate and faithful description of the battle they had ever yet heard or read"—

THE BATTLE OF LAKE ERIE.

Come ye, whose feet old Erie kindly laves,
And join to pour an anthem o'er her waves,
This day to her broad breast she calls the Free,
And bids them welcome to her Jubilee.

Thou stately Queen of all the lordly lakes
Down where Niagara's thundering chorus breaks,
Snatch forth a strain of Nature's lofty praise
To swell the chant thy sister Cities raise.
Come, thou old Erie, worthy of thy name,
Bearing the trophy of thy hero's fame,—
The fragments of that torn and shattered wreck
With battle's foot-prints still upon the deck;
And thou, too, ancient "City of the Straits,"
Bring forth the guns that once assailed thy gates.
Tho' rude and harmless now they seem to be,
They once were leveled at thy liberty.
And thou, fair Forest City, gliding from thy grove,
Come like the swan and o'er the waters move.
And coy Sandusky, nestled in thy bay,
Where lovers dream the evening hours away,
Come with Monroe from River Raisin's shore
And proud Toledo, valiant as of yore;
Come, grave Maumee, for years full widely known,
By Heroes, and a fever all thine own;—
Come one, come all, young men and maidens come,
With streaming banners and the rattling drum,
Extend thy peace-clad galleys far and wide,
And deck with pennants all the heaving tide.
Come with your Steamers, each in grand array,
Come with glad hearts to celebrate this day,
And loudly let the brazen cannon play!

'Tis not of scenes at Salamis we sing,
Nor brazen prows led by some Roman King;

Not *Drake*, who, bursting like a Northern gale
Upon the dread Armada's myriad sail,
Broke up and scattered on th' avenging sea
The power that struck at Albion's liberty;
Nor *him* to whom were given the massive keys
That first unlocked our dark Hesperian seas,
That grand old sea-king, sent and led of God,
To kiss with foreign keel our virgin sod;
Not Nelson struggling on the bloody brine
To carve great England's name on Ocean's shrine;
Nor brave Paul Jones, who scourged the English seas,
The winged herald of our liberties.
Nor Lawrence, who, when life was on the slip,
Still bravely cried, " Pray, don't give up the ship."
'Tis none of these whose mighty deeds we sing,
But one to whom the Nation's heart will cling
Till Erie rolls no wave to either shore,
An old Niagara's voice be heard no more:
The MAN, who five and forty years ago,
Here, on these waves, then tinged with crimson glow,
'Mid crashing spars, and War's wild overthrow,
Laid proud old England's blood-red pennant low.
Let all our Cities in one common Hymn
Send PERRY's praise around old Erie's brim,
PERRY the young, PERRY the bold and brave,
THE CHRISTIAN HERO of our common wave;
Let all the bugles their best music pour,
Let all the cannon in glad triumph roar,
And let their echoes, leaping from each shore,
> Still chime his name,
> And lofty fame,
Forever, and forever more!

Slow creeps to birth the opening Autumn day,
Slow breaks along the Lake his herald ray,
The birds not yet from out the forest raise
In chorus clear, their matin hymn of praise—
Still sleeps the duck upon the quiet flood,
Still weeps the tinted maple of the wood;
Not e'en the mournful cry of waking loon
Has yet ascended to the sinking moon;

Nor night scarce lifted from the misty deep
The sable mantle of great Nature's sleep;
When circled round this lonely island-bay,
The British hulls like drowsy dragons lay—
Bright glow the colors round their bulwarks spread,
Bright beams their snowy canvas overhead;
Softly their ensigns open on the air,
Compact their lines, their brazen metal bare—
" *Sail ho! Sail ho!* " sounds from the mast-head high,
And thro' the slumbering fleet, the startling cry
Calls out from bunk and berth, the ready crew,
To find their leader's orders all in view;
For, see! his signals on the dawn display,
" *The foe in sight—let all be under way!* "

Now trumpets hoarse along the waters speak,
And block and tackle thro' each vessel creak;
The sailor's deep-toned chimes in chorus fall
Responsive to the boatswain's piping call;
As thro' the fleet, goes up with clam'rous joy,
The shout, " *all hands trip anchor, and ahoy!* "

Now slowly glide the vessels under way,
And point their prows beyond the silent bay;—
" *Yon isle, pass to the left!* " their Leader cries,
" *It is not safe!* " the Sailing Mate replies;
" *Then to the right! for I this very day
Am full resolved to meet the enemy!* "
And with the wind then filling up his sail,
He leads the fleet tow'rd War's descending gale.
And while the vessels onward slowly drag,
Lo! upward mounts brave Perry's fighting flag;
And soon the noisy music of the drum
Commands " *all hands to quarters!* " and they come—
Sealed are the hatches, and the lint outspread
To staunch the wounded, and enshroud the dead—
And Surgeons with their aids, descend and wait
For such as here may pass Death's bloody gate—

Upon the flag-ship of the royal fleet
Stands one who erst had fought at Nelson's feet,

Who in the bloody fight at Trafalgar
Had bravely won an honorable scar,
Coldly he looks, (and with that high disdain
Which Albion loves to wear when on the main,)
On that raw fleet now straggling from the bay,
Led by a youth who on that deadly day
First mingled in the sea-fight's wild affray—
His vessels framed along the wood-clad shore
Had scarcely dipped the wave which onward bore
Their dauntless builder to the battle's roar—
Young were his years, but all his bearing told
That he a Warrior's wisdom could unfold
When e'er the struggle of the day should come,
And shot and shell began to thunder home.

Slow wore the day, each Captain's skillful eye
Seeking to weather-gage his enemy.
The winds were hushed—hushed was each sailor's breath,
Ere the mad guns expelled their blast of death;
Signals were flashing through each battle line,
And gun-boats dashing to obey the sign.
Silence hung heavy o'er the emerald wave,
That silence which so sorely tries the brave,
And ere it ushers in the battle-cry,
Gives visions to the home returning eye,
And whispers to each heart, *what if thou die!*
Or like the hurricane's mysterious hush
That sleeps upon the air, before the rush
Of overturning winds, and tempest blast
That down to Earth both tower and turret cast.

Eight bells had pealed the full meridian hour
As battle's gloomy front began to lower.
Set were the sails,—set every sailor's lip,
On board each fair and slow-advancing ship;
And with the proper range each crew now runs,
Through every port-hole all the black mouthed guns.
From out the rigging, as their vision cleared,
The eager look outs with their glasses peered.
" *What see'st in yon fleet?*" the Briton cries,
" *I see the crew at prayers,*" a tar replies—

" *At prayers!*" says one, with mocking laugh and jeer,
" *I'd rather hear the rebels curse and swear!*"
" *At prayers,*" another said; " *such men I fear;*
" *Perhaps the Nation's God those prayers may hear!*
" *And woe to those who meet* HIS GLITTERING SPEAR!"

Closer, still closer, creep the squadrons on,
Nearer, yet nearer, frowns the shotted gun—
And now the sea bird's wild, prophetic scream,
(As o'er the waves his snowy pinions gleam,)
A moment starts each palpitating crew,
And bids all hearts express the last adieu.

But see that silver wreath of curling smoke,—
'Tis Barclay's gun! The silence now is broke.
CHAMPLIN, with rapid move and steady eye,
Sends back in thunder tones a bold reply.
Another gun! another thunders out,
And hark! there goes the British battle-shout,
And hark again! above the pealing roar,
" *Close order, men! let slip the dogs of war!*"
'Tis PERRY's trumpet speaks, and thro' the fleet
His guns, unmuzzled, pour their iron sleet,
And soon, with battle's blaze, begin to heat.
" Close action," was the order of the day,
And down mid gathering smoke, and fire, and spray,
The " Lawrence" fearless holds her deadly way.

Bravely she met the storm of iron hail,
That swept her decks and splintered every rail;
Three hostile vessels crowding hard and fast,
Poured, through her bulwarks, War's destructive blast;
And as each spar, and brace, and bowline fell,
And men lay shattered by the crashing shell,
She seemed almost the very prey of Hell!
Muzzle to muzzle still she poured her fire,
Though every minute saw a life expire—
And when unbroken limbs had ceased to be
And none remained erect on foot or knee,
The wounded men came crawling from below
To pull a rope or let a lanyard go.

One gun was left upon her starboard side—
'Twas all she had to stem War's dreadful tide;
This PERRY seized—and with a lighted brand,
Discharged a shot with his ensanguined hand,
For now, alas! the scuppers held most all his bleeding band!

Stripped of her spars, and shorn of every sail,
The "Lawrence" lay a wreck before the gale;
Her guns disabled, and without a crew,
What could her still unconquered Captain do?
He yields to Yarnall his poor shattered wreck,
And points his way tow'rd the Niagara's deck;
Behold, he leaves the vessels splintered side,
To drive his boat across the bloody tide,—
With flag in hand and close-compressed lip,
He tells brave Yarnall "Don't give up the ship!"
Then bids the coxswain let the painter slip.
Now, bolt upright he stands, although the sky
Seems raining leaden bullets on his way;
Until his men, all over-anxious grown,
Among the stern-sheets drag the Hero down.

The gauntlet pass'd—now all his sailors' eyes
Turn to the ship where his proud ensign flies,
Then, louder than the roaring cannon's voice,
They lift the cheer, and with glad hearts rejoice;
For, though around him War's dread volley flew,
The God of Battle safely led him through—
Gave to his hand another gallant craft,
And sent a breeze his ownward way to waft,
A moment more, and on he wildly drives,
While all his battle-thirst again revives.
Grand as Leonidas at Thermopylæ,
Dashed now our Hero on the enemy;
Full armed, once more in thunderbolts he falls,
And pours his broadside on their wooden walls;
The gun-boats roar along his bloody wake,
And like young demons, rend the lines they break.
Flash after flash his fatal lightnings shone,
Crash after crash he brings their canvas down—
Groan after groan succeeded every gun,

Moan followed moan, until the work was done—
A squadron lost, and Perry's victory won!

Yes! the great battle now at last is done!
Hush'd are the shoutings, hush'd is every gun;
Down run the ensigns of Great England's Might!
Down drops her star athwart the gloomy night!
Brave BARCLAY, fainting at his sore defeat,
His sword surrenders, with his broken fleet;
While upward leap the glorious stripes and stars,
And well adorn the Briton's shattered spars.
Loud shout our heroes at each heated gun,
" A battle and a name this day is won!
And England's triumph on the sea is done!"

Brave Perry, gathering now the victor's spoils,
Sadly and slowly tow'rd the harbor toils;
Bright were his eyes, though sad his pensive mood,
As he beheld his scuppers run with blood;
Or saw afloat upon the crimsoned wave,
Some face, that e'en in death, revealed a brave.
His heart was tender, and he mourned the death
Of those who served him with their latest breath;
And with a tear and prayer his dead he lay
Within the shade of this sweet island-bay,
And here, through Autumn's melancholy days,
Old Erie sobs, and chants their endless praise.

Here too the foe, in slow procession come,
With wailing trumpets, and with muffled drum;
The plaintive music sweeps the harbor's walls,
And out upon the lake its echo falls,
Where War's dark cloud still hugs the trembling wave,
And spreads her mantle o'er the sailor's grave;
While every soldier, every sailor heart
Forgets his flag, and acts out Nature's part;
Walks slowly by the rude but bannered bier,
And give's his foe the honest warrior's tear.
And there beneath yon willow's waving bough,
The foes of yesterday, are brothers now.

This day from Lake-washed cities here we throng
To raise anew the chivalrous battle song,
To see again the battering squadron's flame,
Again to hear the cannon loud proclaim
Their thundering pæans to great Perry's name—
To meet the remnants of his glorious band
And grasp with more than grateful hand,
CHAMPLIN and BLAIR, BROWNELL and PARSONS pure!
Long may their waning strength and years endure.
New generations here this day we see
With brilliant pomp and gay festivity,
With lute and tabret and the vocal chime,
That rings far down the avenues of Time,
With brazen trump and clanging drum and bell,
In soul-refreshing strains again to tell
       How well,
       How bravely well,
         Great Perry stood
       When shot and shell
       Around him fell,
And vexed and seethed old Erie's peaceful flood.
And dyed her emerald waves with Valor's precious blood.

But more! we come this day with grateful thanks,
To crown this classic island's wooded banks
With broad foundation stones, on which to rear
The thrilling record of that glorious year,—
To write on high old Erie's Naval story,
AND GIVE TO GOD, AND PERRY ALL THE GLORY!

Yes! let the monumental shaft arise
Above these forest boughs and greet the skies;
Here let the woodland birds each morning raise
To Perry, and his braves, their hymn of praise.
Here let the Nation come with each glad year
And yield this dust the tributary tear;
Here wreathe the Autumn cup, and loud proclaim
Fresh honors to our Hero's honored name,—
Here chant, how Man the very Fates can bend
By bravely *persevering to the end.*
'Twas this that won for Perry his renown,

'Tis this that plucks from Tyranny her crown,
'Tis this that saves our flag on Land and Sea,
And girds with sentinels of Liberty
This teeming land—God keep it ever free !

Then let us send the towering shaft on high,
To court new blessings from each morning sky;
To teach our rising youth on land and flood,
That Liberty is worthy of their blood;
And on its tablet write, in boldest line,
Those words that round this Lake should ever shine—
That modest message of our Hero's pen,—
Long may it live among our Naval men,
Long gleam from all our armed forts and towers,
"WE'VE MET THE ENEMY, AND THEY ARE OURS !"

Hon. Judge Mason, of Toledo, was next introduced. We regret to say this gentleman's remarks were almost wholly lost upon his hearers, as what with the whistling of steamers, firing of salutes, beating of drums, ringing of bells, &c., his audience were in a measure deafened. We are, therefore, unable to lay before our readers a satisfactory report of the gentleman's speech, which we regret very much.

INCIDENTS OF THE BATTLE.

The discourse on the Battle of Lake Erie by Dr. Usher Parsons, being written by an eye witness of high character and intelligence, is the most authentic history that we have of that day. From this discourse, delivered before the Rhode Island Historical Society, in 1852, we extract the following passages, as giving a graphic picture of what was going on in the Lawrence:

Among those early brought down was Lieut. Brooks, son of the late Governor of Massachusetts, a most accomplished gentlemen and officer; and renowned for personal beauty. A cannon-ball had struck him in the hip, he knew his doom, and inquired how long he should live; I told him a few hours. He inquired two or three times how the day was going, and expressed a hope that the Commodore would be spared. But new-comers from deck brought more and more dismal reports, until finally it was announced that we had struck. In the wailings of despair among the wounded, some of whom were for sinking the ship, I lost sight of poor Brooks for a few minutes, but when the electrifying cry was heard that the enemy's two ships had struck, I rushed on deck to see if it were true, and then to poor Brooks to cheer him; but he was no more,—he was too much exhausted by his wounds to survive the confusion that preceded this happy transition.

When the battle was raging most severely, Midshipman Laub came down, with his arm badly fractured; I applied a splint, and requested him to go forward and lie down. As he was leaving me, and while my hand was on him, a cannon-ball struck him in the side, and dashed against the other side of the room, instantly terminating his sufferings. Another person was killed, and one wounded in the Surgeon's room, and six cannon-balls passed through this room in a line of ten feet, and all of them between three and four feet from the floor.

There were other incidents less painful to witness. The Commodore's dog had seated himself in the bottom of the closet containing all our crockery. A cannon-ball passed through the closet, and smashed crockery and door, covering the floor with fragments. The dog set up a barking protest against the right of such an invasion of his chosen retirement.

Lieut. Yarnall had his scalp badly torn and came below with the blood streaming over his face. Some lint was hastily applied and confined with a large bandanna, with directions to report himself for better dressing, after the battle, as he insisted on returning to the deck. The cannon-balls had knocked to pieces the hammocks stowed away on deck, and let loose their contents, which were reed or flag tops, that floated in the air like feathers, and gave the appearance of a snow storm. These lighted on Yarnall's head covered with blood, and coming below with another injury, his bloody face covered with cat-tails, made his head resemble that of a huge owl. Some of the wounded roared out with laughter, "That the Devil had come for us." At half-past 2 o'clock, out of one hundred and one sound men, wherewith the Lawrence had gone into action, twenty-two were killed, and sixty-one wounded, a slaughter unprecedented in naval warfare! Her rigging was shot away —her spars were splintered, her sails torn to pieces, her guns dismounted; she lay a helpless wreck on the water. Capt. Perry had himself just assisted to fire her last gun. He ordered the boat to be lowered; and saying to his first Lieutenant, Mr. Yarnall—who though severely wounded, refused to stay below,—"I leave to your discretion to strike or not—but the American colors must not come down over my head to-day." He took the battle flag upon his shoulder, and descended into the boat. A few minutes later the Lawrence was compelled to strike her colors.

As the American colors came down, there went up from the British snips a shout of triumph. To one Wilson Mays, on board the Lawrence, the Master, Mr. Taylor, said—" Go below, Mays, you are too weak to be here." "I can do something, sir." "What can you do?" " I can sound the pumps, sir, and let a strong man go to the guns;" and when the fight was ended, there he was found with a ball through his heart.

The following song, for some time subsequent to the Battle, was quite current among the sailors, and was thought proper to be introduced here for preservation, as a relic of the times :—

BATTLE OF ERIE, 1813.

Avast, honest Jack, now before you get mellow,
Come tip us that stave just, my hearty old fellow,
'Bout the young Commodore, and his fresh water crew,
Who keel-hauled the Britons and captured a few.

" 'Twas just at sun-rise, and a glorious day,
Our squadron at anchor snug in Put-in-Bay,
When we saw the bold Britons, and clear for a bout,
Instead of put in, by the Lord we put out.

" Up went Union Jack, never up there before,
' Don't give up the ship!' was the motto it bore;
And as soon as that motto our gallant men saw,
They thought of their Lawrence and shouted huzza!

" O! then it would have raised your hat three inches higher,
To see how we dashed in among them like fire!
The Lawrence went first and the rest as they could,
And a long while the brunt of the action she stood.

" 'Twas peppering work—fire, fury and smoke,
And groans that from wounded lads spite of 'em broke.
The water grew red round our ship as she lay,
Though 'twas never before so, till that bloody day.

" They fell all around me like spars in a gale;
The shot made a sieve of each rag of a sail;
And out of our crew scarce a dozen remained;
But these gallant tars still the battle maintained.

" 'Twas then our commannder—God bless his young heart,
Thought it best from his well-peppered ship to depart,
And bring up the rest, who were tugging behind—
For why—they were sadly in want of a wind.

" So to Yarnall he gave the command of his ship,
And set out like a lark, on this desperate trip,
In a small open sail, right through their whole fleet,
Who with many a broad-side our cock-boat did greet.

" I steered her, and damme if every inch
Of these timbers of mine at each crack didn't flinch:
But our tight little commodore, cool and serene,
To stir ne'er a muscle by any was seen.

" Whole volleys of muskets were levelled at him,
But the devil a one ever grazed e'en a limb,
Though he stood up aloft in the stern of the boat
Till the crew pulled him down by the skirt of his coat.

" At last, thro' Heaven's mercy we reached t'other ship,
And the wind springing up we gave her the whip,
And run down their line, boys, thro' thick and thro' thin,
And bothered their crews with a horrible din.

" Then starboard and larboard, and this way and that,
We banged them and raked them, and laid their masts flat,
Till one, after t'other, they hauled down their flag,
And an end, for that time, put to Jonny Bull's brag.

" The Detroit and Queen Charlotte and Lady Provost:
Not able to fight or run, gave up the ghost:
And not one of them all from our graplings got free,
Tho' we'd fifty-four guns and they just sixty-three.

"Smite my limbs! but they got their bellies full then,
And found what it was, boys, to buckle with men,
Who fight, or what's just the same, think that they fight
For their country's free trade, and their own native right.

" Now give us a bumper to Elliott and those
Who came up in good time to belabour our foes;
To our fresh water sailors we'll top off one more,
And a dozen, at least, to our young Commodore.

" And though Britains may brag of their ruling the ocean,
And that sort of thing, by the Lord I've a notion,
I'll bet all I'm worth—who takes it, who takes?
Tho' their lords of the sea, we'll be lords of the lakes!"

INCIDENTS OF THE CELEBRATION.

Loud calls being made for Ossian E. Dodge, at the close of Dr. Parson's address, Gov. Chase stepped forward and remarked :

" It is with no little gratification that I am enabled to state that we will now have an original song by an original singer! That the song is good, and will be well sung, you will be well assured when I inform you that it will be sung by the author Ossian E. Dodge." Three hearty cheers were now given for Mr. Dodge, when that gentleman came forward with the " Barker Family" to assist him in the chorus; and just as he was about commencing,—the Governor again arose and remarked:

"Though our singer's name is Dodge, and it is a *common dodge* of his to *dodge* out an original song in a few minutes time,—we are happy to know that he hasn't on this occasion *dodged us.*" Shouts of laughter followed, but Mr. Dodge quickly replied.

"If—as it has been stated—I am in the habit of hastily dodging at songs, I hope whenever our worthy Chairman is present—that my songs, may be truly *Chase-d.*" Amid peals of laughter, Mr. Dodge now commenced the following song, and was vociferously cheered at the end of each verse.

WE'VE MET THE ENEMY AND THEY'RE OURS.

Just forty-five years now have fled
Since Perry young and bold,
Fought bravely and for Freedom bled,
And thus his victory told.

CHORUS.

Hurrah! hurrah! tra la la, la la la,
We live for music, love and flowers;
Hurrah! hurrah! tra la la, la la la,
We've met the enemy and they're ours.

Applause or praise with flattering tongue
Brave Perry ne'er did court;
But when the victory he had won
This was his plain report.
Chorus.

When e'er opponents of the free
Are on our waters found,
Our gallant sons of Liberty
Will thus the air resound.
Chorus.

But now with England we're at peace
And free from toil and care,
We'll strive the Union to increase
And fill with strains the air.
Chorus.

Our love for peace and brotherhood
Comes from the God above,
For evil we should render good,
And conquer all with love.
Chorus.

ON BOARD THE STEAMER OCEAN.　THE RETURN.

On casting off, the steamers kept together in the Bay for some time, whilst the bands kept up a constant playing, gun answered gun from the steamers and from the shore, and cheer answered cheer from the crowded boats. Finally, with a parting cheer, the steamers separated and headed for home.

It having been noticed that Mr. Dodge was busily writing a song du-

ring the exercises on the stand, he was loudly called for at the close of
Judge Mason's remarks to sing his "machine song," but excusing himself on the ground of not having sufficiently strong lungs to successfully
compete with six steamboat bells, and as many more engine whistles,
he promised to sing the song on the steamer Ocean,—claiming that that
would be a more appropriate place—inasmuch as the song contained a
history of the entire day's proceedings. On being called for on the
boat, Mr. Dodge said that he hoped no one would criticise the song as a
poetical composition—for although in business life the motto was "measures not men"—with a rhyming machine under full headway it was
quite the reverse—being "men not measure." Here it is:—

DODGE'S MACHINE SONG.

'Tis oftentimes said that a rhyming machine,
Is a novel invention, not every day seen;
But bringing to-day quite an old one along,
I'll set the mill going and grind out a song.

Well, just at the half past seven o'clock,
The good steamer Ocean pulled out from the dock,
And while from the river she merrily ran on
The ladies all screamed at the sound of the cannon.

There were plenty of soldiers with musket and sword,
And a number of men lost their hats overboard,
While soon in the cabin we all had a chance
To each take a lady and all have a dance.

And now I will this opportunity take
To say that steam boats are well manned on the lake;
And you will no doubt all respond to my motion
That none can be more so than good steamer Ocean.

To prove that this steamer is rapid and fierce,
She's got for an agent one General Pierce.
And passengers dream of the cupids and heavens,
While sailing so smoothly with good Capt. Evans.

When the steamer is ready and all wish to start her,
The clerk sells the tickets—one good David Carter;
And to be doubly sure that she'll never be late,
One William McKay is the popular mate.

Of danger there never can be any fear
So long as George Watson is chief engineer;
And no one to grumble can ever be able
When the stewart, John Greensdale, provides for the table.

While sailing along seven miles from the main,
There suddenly rose quite a drizzling rain,
When a man who was just on the invalid list
Said he wished from his heart that the storm might be *missed.*

The storm passing over, the weather proved fair—
'Twas thought through the means of a minister's prayer—
And soon into harbor we easily ran
Amid deafening cheers from the ship Michigan.

On the Forest Queen coming there sprung up a race,
To get the first view of our Governor Chase,
And to see 'em all running was no little sport,
While the cannon kept booming their splendid report.

On getting together and mounting the stand,
We were stilled by the chief magistrate of the land;
And then brother Duffield soon offered a prayer,
And proffered his thanks that the weather was fair.

And next the large crowd with the happiest face
Paid the best of attention to Governor Chase;
He welcomed old soldiers, all men and their babies,
And welcomed most heartily all of the ladies.

Sandusky next gave us her venerable Cooke,
   And though he was feeble yet talked like a book;
He said we had all of us cause to be merry
While thinking of valorous Commodore Perry.

Capt. Champlin who thought he could write to you better,
Next gave to the crowd a most capital letter;
When brave Capt. Brownell, whom none can impeach,
With tears in his eyes gave a capital speech.

The good Surgeon Parsons next rose on the stand
And gave us account of the Commodore's band;
He caused his old comrades to shed many tears,
And brought from the audience nine hearty cheers.

The next man to mention in this lengthy ditty,
Was the honorable Mayor from our own Forest City,
Who spoke very eloquent, feeling and loud,
And plainly with eloquence carried the crowd.

Just forty-five years have departed, my friends,
Since England found out that she must make amends,
And the lords of that country will ever remember
Young Commodore Perry and the Tenth of September.

Our Good " Father Gidding's" of venerable worth,
By the call of the crowd was obliged to come forth,
And with warm, honest heart, and with eloquence good
He stirred up the people and heated their blood.

Judge Wilkin's, an aged and comical man,
Next handsomely spoke for the State Michigan,
And his whole speech with humor and eloquence rung
That the pride of Toledo should ever be sung.

Friend Duffield now rose, and perhaps you all know him,
Who read us a witty and capital poem;
He pictured the battle quite vivid and terse,
And did it quite handsomely all up in verse.

The screech of the pipes blowing steam in the basin,
Proved rather too much for Toledo Mason;
When the crowd without stopping to render their vote,
Made a rapid stampede for their favorite boat.

I've come down at last to the end of the list,
And the mill must now stop for want of a grist;
For the mill requires feeding as every one knows,
So the ditty is now brought at last to a close.

Three rousing cheers were given for Mr. Dodge at the conclusion, and he was requested to repeat the song which had been given at the platform on the Island.

ON BOARD THE STEAMER QUEEN CITY.

While the steamer was passing out of Sandusky Bay, with three of the survivors of the Battle on board, Dr. Usher Parsons recognized and pointed out the locality where the fleet had come to anchor, a few days before the engagement, and fired three guns, a signal previously agreed upon between Capt. Perry and Gen. Harrison. The next day the General and his suite came on board drenched with rain, among whom were the celebrated Gov. McArthur and Hon. Lewis Cass, and also a number of Indian chiefs. Here they received the volunteer reinforcements from the army. A day or two after their reception on board, the General and Staff were saluted with the usual number of guns. They stood during the time on the quarter deck of the Lawrence in full dres uniform, and the Doctor remarked that he has never since looked upon a nobler and more martial staff of officers. When the firing began, the "Indian Braves" dodged below in double quick time, and remained in the cabin until it ceased. Their ears were unused to such kind of thunder.

As it was known that our Cleveland friends had their "Bard" on board the Ocean, and the Detroiters the "distinguished poet of the day" on the May Queen, it was suggested, during the return of the Queen City, that "Sandusky" ought also to be represented by the Muses, whereupon one of her citizens became rhapsodical, and subsequently produced the following:

THE ISLANDS OF ERIE.

BY R. R. MCMEENS, M. D.

The Islands of Erie, arrayed in full dress,
Enrobe the lake scene with a strange loveliness.

As gorgeously decked in bright verdure they lie,
In the soft mellow haze of a still Autumn sky.
No more brilliant gems though lauded they be
Ever gleamed mid the groups of old Grecian sea.
They circle the storm-brewing gates of the West;
To soothe the "Mad Spirit"* of Erie to rest,
And lend their slight forms to the rage of the sea.
To shelter the storm-tossed in succoring lee;
Or like sentinels seem to be pointing the way
To the harboring arms of bold "Put-in-Bay."

When the winds breathless sleep in their caverns of peace
How sylph-like they sit on the lake's lucent face;
Or mirrored in beauty on crimson dyed wave
When the sun silent sinks in his gold-tinted grave,
And the purple horizon, depends as a shroud,
Of tapestried mantle, in folds of rich cloud,
Then deep'ning so gently upon the pale glow,
So sombre and sad, scarce seeming to know,
When the last flitting ray of fading twilight,
Merges in darkness and death gloom of night.

Oh! Islands of Erie, how many a scene
Of shipwreck and battle around you have been.
How many a gallant young hero went down,
When Perry and sailors won glorious renown.
You stand as proud monuments over the dead,
Who sleep at thy feet in their coffinless bed;
While the winds shriek or whisper a requiem sigh,
And the waves join in murmuring a fond lullaby,
And the Mariner gliding along by thy side,
Recounts all their deeds with emotions of pride.

Oh! Islands of beauty, on Erie's broad breast
That smile in the sunshine like havens of rest;
Or when the Storm-God in his wrath wildly raves,
Like "Sisters"† of mercy hang over the waves,
Ever bloom in your freshness as lovely as now,
To enrapture the eye and make the heart glow.

---

*Erie in the Indian tongue signifies "Mad Spirit."
†The westernmost group are named the "Three Sisters."

All ordinary communications, pertaining to matter connected with the
Monument Association should be addressed to the Secretary, and those
of a business and financial character to W. S. Pierson, Esq., Treasurer,
both of Sandusky City, Ohio.

R. R. McMEENS, M. D., Secretary.